Storm Rescue

DARREL and
SALLY ODGERS

Illustrated by
JANINE DAWSON

Kane Miller
A DIVISION OF EDC PUBLISHING

For Maureen Odgers Turner – a lovely
person to know
- Darrel and Sally O

To Rosemary & Alan
- Janine Dawson

First American Edition 2017
Kane Miller, A Division of EDC Publishing

Text copyright © Sally and Darrel Odgers 2015
Cover copyright © Scholastic Australia 2015
Internal illustrations copyright © Janine Dawson 2015
First published by Scholastic Press a division of Scholastic Australia Pty Limited in 2015.
Cover illustration by Heath McKenzie
This edition published under license from Scholastic Australia Pty Limited

For information contact:
Kane Miller, A Division of EDC Publishing
PO Box 470663
Tulsa, OK 74147-0663
www.kanemiller.com
www.edcpub.com
www.usbornebooksandmore.com

Library of Congress Control Number: 2016959845

Printed and bound in the United States of America

1 2 3 4 5 6 7 8 9 10

ISBN: 978-1-61067-657-1

Dear Readers,

My name is **Barnaby Station Stamp of Approval**, but you can call me Stamp. My friend Ace and I travel around the country with James Barnaby in a vehicle we call the **Fourby**. I am a **border collie**, so you won't be surprised to learn that I am handsome and clever. Ace isn't a border collie, but she's clever, too. James says her second name is Trouble.

James talks to us a lot. Often he talks to Ace and me when other humans are around. He says if they don't understand that, then that is their problem, not his.

The story you are about to read is our third big Pup Patrol adventure. We were camped at the K9 Festival when Cyclone Julia hit . . .

Yours,
Stamp
Pup Patroller

Who's Who.

The Crew of the Fourby

James Barnaby. James is 19. He wants to be a vet.

Barnaby Station Stamp of Approval. Me. A clever, handsome border collie.

Ace. A dog of mixed breed and bad manners.

Other Family and Friends

Dad and Mum Barnaby. James's parents back at Barnaby Station.

Tina. A friend who lives in Jasper.

Pipwen. Tina's border collie puppy.

At Atherton Tops

Jay and Hayley. Stewards at Atherton Tops.

Imogen. Their daughter.

Maureen and Blue. A handler and her blue heeler.

Mr. Grig. A visitor at the K9 Festival.

Tilly. His terrier mix.

Stamp's Glossary

Barnaby Station Stamp of Approval.
Pedigreed animals often have long names.
My parents are named Barnaby Station Penny
Black and Brightwood Superlative.

Border collies. Herding dogs that came from
the Anglo-Scottish borders. They are one of the
most intelligent dogs in the world.

The Fourby. Four-wheel drive SUV.

Chapter One
North to Adventure

Ace was missing. I *had* to find her.

I sniffed around and soon found her trail. All the other dog smells had washed away in the storm so it was easy to track her. I trotted along and started to feel confident. *I can do this!* I told myself.

I trotted past broken vans and torn tents towards where we had camped. Ace had come this way. She must have been looking for the Fourby.

That's when I saw the huge tree we had parked under. It had blown down in the cyclone and now it lay smashed and broken all over the ground. And Ace's trail headed straight for it.

So, why was I hunting for Ace after the cyclone?

It all started when James entered a race called the **City2Surf**.

Dogs aren't allowed to run in the City2Surf, so James asked his aunt and uncle to look after Ace and me. Ace whined the whole time. She wanted James, not other people.

"Sometimes we have to stay with someone else," I said. "We should behave well so James will be proud of us."

Ace squinted at me and said, "Gnaaaghh!" She said it again when Aunt asked her to stop digging on the armchair. Then she dug even faster so that her front paws were a blur.

When James came back from his race he was grinning from ear to ear. "I can't wait to do it again!" he said. "I've already signed up for another race."

I **suppaws** I looked sulky. I know Ace did. James scrubbed our ears and laughed.

"It's okay. The next race I've entered

is for dogs as well. There are all sorts of activities and a huge challenge race with ladders and water and high balance beams."

"That sounds dangerous," said Aunt.

"No, no, it's really well organized," said James. "It's the Great Atherton K9 and Friends Festival up at Atherton Tops."

"Is that in Queensland?" asked Uncle.

James nodded. "In the Far North. We've never been to Queensland. It'll be *great!*"

"It'll be hot," said Aunt.

James put two dining chairs back-to-back and balanced Aunt's ironing board across them. Then he showed Aunt and Uncle how I could jump onto one chair, walk across the board and jump down the other side safely.

Ace wanted some attention so she dug at the armchair again.

"Ace, stop that," said James.

Ace stopped and **smarled**. James snuggled her. "Good girl!"

I don't think Aunt and Uncle were sorry when we all got back in the Fourby and headed north. Aunt and Uncle are not used to dogs that dig on chairs.

Ace sat in the backseat. I sat next to James. That's because James trusts me not to **yaffle** whenever I see a rabbit.

Ace scratched at the back of my seat. "Are we there yet?"

"No," I said.

Every day, we stuck our noses out the windows and sniffed new scents. Every night, we camped in a different place. When Ace thought it was time for a walk, she whined in the high-pitched, annoying way James calls *nose-whinging*. "Eeee!" Then James would stop the Fourby and take us for a run.

One day we were playing chase-the-stick near a beach campsite when someone called out. "James! James Barnaby!"

It was Tina, the girl we met during our second Pup Patrol adventure.

"Hi!" she said. "I saw the Fourby at the campsite. I thought it must be you." She bent to pat Ace and me. "Are you taking Stamp and Ace to the K9 Festival?"

"Yes," said James. "We're really looking forward to the endurance challenge race."

"I'm on my way to pick up a pony, but I'm going to the festival first," said Tina.

"Don't you need a dog to enter?" asked James.

Tina laughed. "I *do* have a dog now. I got her a couple of weeks ago."

Of-paws, Ace and I already knew Tina was traveling with a dog. We smelled it when she patted us.

"She's asleep in the van," added Tina. "I'll introduce you later." Then she waved good-bye and headed back to camp.

Ace barked at the waves and got salt water up her nose. Then she tried to catch a seagull.

"Missed," I said, as it flew away.

Splat!

Ace might have missed the seagull, but the seagull didn't miss Ace. James had to give her a bath when we went back to camp!

Stamp's Glossary

City2Surf. An eight-mile running race for humans, held in Sydney, Australia.

Nose-whinging. A really annoying high-pitched whine.

Of-paws. Of course, for dogs.

Smarl. A dog grin. Some dogs smarl a lot. Some don't do it at all.

Suppaws. Suppose, for dogs.

Yaffle. Noisy yapping and barking. Small dogs do this when they are overexcited.

Chapter Two

Storm Warning

Tina's new dog, Pipwen, was a border collie like me, but a lot younger. She was a puppy, about ten weeks old. She wagged her fluffy tail at us and tried to lick Ace's face. Ace **muttered** at her.

I gave Pipwen a **nose-over**. "Hello, pup," I said.

"Hello, nice big dog," said Pipwen, bouncing. "Hello, not-nice little dog."

Ace lifted her lip to show her sharp

fangs. "Stay away from Stamp, puppy."

I sighed. Ace was being **pawsessive**.

James picked up Pipwen and snuggled her, and *I* felt pawsessive.

"She's a good-looking pup," said James.

"Yes. Her pedigree name is Trumpben Pippi's Wednesday. She's too young to enter any events this year, but the festival will be a good chance to **socialize** her."

"I hope it might be a good place to socialize Ace, too," said James. "She didn't behave very well at my aunt and uncle's place. Have you been to Atherton Tops before?"

"No, but I've been to Far North Queensland," said Tina. "It's very hot."

"That's what my aunt said." James grinned. "But we don't mind a bit of sunshine."

The next afternoon, James used our **HF radio** to talk to Dad Barnaby back home at Barnaby Station.

"Hi, James," said Dad Barnaby. "Where are you now? Over."

"We're on our way to Atherton Tops in Far North Queensland. Over."

"Did you know there's a cyclone warning for that area? **Cyclone Julia** is coming in from the ocean. I'd probably wait a week or so before going north. You'll be safer if you go inland. Over."

"Thanks for the warning, Dad. Say hi to Mum. Over."

"Will do," said Dad Barnaby. "Take care, James."

James ended the call and sighed. "If we wait a week, we'll miss the festival. I suppose they'll cancel it, though. You can't run races in a cyclone."

We got back into the Fourby and drove inland. "I hope Tina knows about the cyclone," James said.

That night, it was too hot to stay in the tent, so we slept under the stars. Even Ace, who likes to sleep under a heap of blanket, found a patch of dry grass instead.

13

The next morning was hot and the
sky looked like a blue sheet. Ace jumped
at a passing bird, but she didn't chase
it. I expect she remembered the seagull
incident.

James went to the campsite office. "Is
there any news about Cyclone Julia?" he
asked the manager.

The man smiled at us. "Yeah, I just
heard a weather report. The warning's
been downgraded. The cyclone is heading
back out to sea," he said.

"Do you think it's safe to go up to Atherton Tops? We're supposed to go to a festival there."

"It should be okay," said the man. "A lot of these warnings don't come to much. Just keep an eye on the forecast. Atherton Tops is high on the Tableland, so it's not as hot up there as it is on the coast."

"Great!" said James. "K9 Festival, here we come!"

Stamp's Glossary

Cyclone Julia. Cyclones have names, like dogs and people.

HF radio. High frequency radio. James's radio is not the kind that plays music. It's the kind people use to talk to one another.

Muttered. A mutter is a tiny growl. Dogs do it when they're grumpy.

Nose-over. A check we pawform with our noses. We dogs can tell a lot by sniffing.

Pawsessive. This is the way dogs feel about their people and their things if they don't want to share.

Socialize. Pups need to meet lots of people and other animals while they are young. This helps them to get along with others.

A Word on Pack Order

A pack is a community of dogs. In every pack, there is an alpha dog. The alpha looks after the pack and makes sure all dogs behave properly. The alpha sometimes gives orders and other dogs have to obey.

When dogs live in a human family, the alpha role should always go to a human. In our Fourby Pack, James is alpha. I am top dog because I have been with James most of my life. Ace is second dog because she has been with us a short time. This works for us. If you have a dog in your family, remember that human/dog packs *must* be led by a human.

Chapter Three

Maureen and Blue

At the foot of the Atherton Tablelands, it was hotter than ever. The air felt wet and heavy. Ace and I panted. Sticking our tongues out is the way dogs cool down. We don't sweat like humans and horses.

"I didn't know it would be *this* hot," James said. "I don't think I can run a race in this weather."

I whined. Ace panted so hard her sides heaved in and out. James poured

water into our bowl. It was as warm as bathwater!

James sighed. "Since we're here, we'd better drive up to Atherton Tops. It's supposed to be cooler there," he said.

The road up to the Tablelands wound around and around and around. I felt as if my nose was pointing the way my tail should go. Ace started nose-whinging.

"Stop it, Ace," said James.

"I feel sick," said Ace. "*Eeee*."

I think we all felt sick. Even though the windows were open, the air was heavy. Up and around we drove until suddenly the road leveled out and stopped winding. We'd reached the top of the **pass.** James parked the Fourby next to a sign with an arrow and a picture of a man running with a dog. James read it aloud.

"The Great Atherton K9 and Friends Festival!"

Ace made a choking noise, so James let her out on the grass. She sat down and pointed her nose at the ground. That's what dogs do when we feel sick. After a bit, she lifted her head and sniffed the air. Her tail came up. "I feel better," she announced.

So did I. The air was fresher here. I heard James take a deep breath. Humans can't smell things nearly as well as dogs, but of-paws they know when air is fresh.

A pickup truck pulled in and parked behind us. The driver and a **blue heeler** got out.

James started talking to the driver. The heeler came over to us. Ace muttered, but I waved my tail.

"*Don't* snarl at him," I told Ace. "Heelers can be grumpy and he's bigger than you."

Ace lifted her lip. "I can be grumpy, too," she said.

The dog looked at us through narrow eyes. "Name's Blue," he said. "Here for the K9 Festival with Maureen, my handler."

"I'm Stamp," I said.

Blue looked at Ace. "Who's the cranky floor mop?"

Ace muttered.

"That's Ace," I said to Blue.

Blue stepped around me to have a good sniff at Ace. "You should teach her better manners," he said.

"Gnaghhhhh," said Ace. "Get your nose out of my face."

Blue barked a laugh. "Settle down, little mop. I used to be a bad dog, too, once. Now I'm a busy dog. Maureen says busy dogs don't have time to be bad. Busy dogs are good and happy."

"We're busy," I assured him. "We're happy, too."

Blue looked hard at Ace, then looked at me.

"Ace is happy, really," I said. "She just enjoys a good grumble."

"I can see that," said Blue. "See you around, Stamp. See you around, Ace." He gave us a quick tail wag and went back to his handler, who was still talking to James.

"I heard that Cyclone Julia went out to sea," he was saying.

Maureen shrugged. "It did, but now it's heading back this way. Cyclones are unpredictable—not even experts know quite what they'll do. Cyclone Julia went back out to sea once, so it might do it again. I'm sure the K9 Festival people

23

will listen to all the weather reports." She looked down at Blue and pointed to the pickup. "Ready, boy?"

Blue trotted over and sat waiting by the door. "You'd better hurry if you want a good camping spot," Maureen said to James. "People and dogs are coming from everywhere."

Stamp's Glossary

Blue heeler. An Australian cattle dog with dingo ancestry.
Pass. Winding road up a hill or mountain.

Chapter Four

Imogen

We drove on to Atherton Tops and joined a long line of vehicles waiting to go through the gates. A tall man with a clipboard wore a T-shirt with the same picture as we'd seen back at the sign.

"I'm James Barnaby," said James. "These are Stamp and Ace."

"Welcome to the festival. I'm Jay Alan." Jay pointed to his T-shirt. "If you need to know anything, ask the people

wearing these shirts."

"Where do we camp?" asked James.

"Find yourself a space over that way."
Jay waved us on to the campground. "Our
main rules are these: Keep your animals
under control. Listen to announcements.
And have a great time!"

"We can do that," said James, but I
saw him glance backward at Ace.

We set up our tent in a clear space between two campers and a huge tree.

The festival was full of people, dogs, cars, tents and a few goats and horses. We went to see the challenge course. There were big pipes lying on their sides to crawl through. There was a long dam with lots of canoes on the bank for the water paddle. There were tall wooden frames with ladders and balance boards.

Workers were busy hammering nails and tying ropes. It all looked and sounded and smelled exciting. I couldn't wait to try it all out.

Ace looked up at one of the ladders.

"I'm *not* climbing that," she said. "I'd fall through the rungs."

"You don't have to," I said. "I'm doing the challenge race with James. You're here to be socialized."

I meant it kindly, but Ace looked annoyed.

As we went back towards the gate, we saw a little girl in overalls with Jay. She had a big smile and short brown hair.

"This is my daughter, Imogen," Jay said. "She's four and loves dogs. Say hi to James, Immo."

"Hi." Imogen pointed at Ace. "What's his name?"

Ace lifted her lip and backed away.

"Her name's Ace," said James.

"Can I pat her?"

Ace lifted the other side of her lip.

"You can pat Stamp," James said. "Ace is a bit . . ." He didn't finish the sentence.

Imogen patted me. She did it properly, putting out her hand so I could sniff it first. She smelled sweet, like apples. "Hello, Stamp," she said. I wagged my tail at her. Then she looked back at Ace. "I still want to pat Ace, too."

Jay laughed. "Immo wants to pat every dog at the festival." He knelt down by his daughter. "You know the rules, Immo. You must never pat any dog unless the owner says it's okay."

"You can pat Ace later," said James. "She's a little cross right now. She felt sick on the winding road."

"I like her," said Imogen. "I have a fort under the big tree. I could play with Ace there. Then she won't be cross."

"Do you play with your own dog in your fort?" asked James.

"I don't have a dog," said Imogen.

"Daddy says I have to wait until I get bigger. And then I'll get a dog like that one." She pointed to Ace.

"You hear that?" said Ace smugly to me. "She likes me."

James turned to Imogen's dad. "Can I help out, Jay?"

"Everything is organized, except for the weather," said Jay. "We're just hoping Cyclone Julia settles down and weakens."

Ace had found something smelly in the grass. Of-paws, she **shoulder-dived** right into it. Then she had a good roll around.

"Yuck, Ace," said James. "Little Immo wouldn't want to pat you now."

James got a bucket from the Fourby and washed Ace. She shook herself all over the tent. Then she went and scrubbed her face dry on James's sleeping bag.

"Oh, *Ace!*" said James and Ace smarled.

When it was nearly bedtime, James called Dad Barnaby.

"Where are you, James? Over," said Dad Barnaby.

"We're at Atherton Tops," said James. "Cyclone Julia went out to sea, so I thought it was safe. It's heading this way again, but everyone says there's nothing to worry about. Over."

"Let's hope they're right," said Dad Barnaby. "Are you near a good solid building? Over."

"There's a huge woolshed and some barns in the next paddock. Over."

"If that cyclone hits, get yourselves and the dogs in the woolshed. Stay inside until it's safe. Do not sit in the Fourby. Stay away from trees. Right? Over."

"Thanks, Dad. Will do."

We had supper with Maureen and

Blue. We were about to settle down for the night when Tina arrived with Pipwen.

"I suppose you heard that cyclone is headed back this way?" said Tina.

James sighed. "Yes. It doesn't seem to know if it's coming or going."

"I hope it's going," said Tina.

Stamp's Glossary

Shoulder-dive. Some dogs like to push their shoulders into smelly things on the ground.

Chapter Five

Attention!

A terrible howling woke us. It was so loud I wanted to cover my ears. Ace scrambled out from under her blanket and started to howl along.

"Ace, stop that," said James sleepily.

Ace didn't stop. Neither did the noise. Instead, it grew louder.

"What *is* that?" James sat up and put his hand around Ace's nose. "Some kind of siren?" He crawled out of the tent.

All around us, people and dogs spilled out of tents and vans. Lots of other dogs barked and howled like Ace. Three goats bolted past, bleating wildly.

Then the siren noise stopped and a **loudspeaker** started up. "Attention, everyone! This is Jay Alan. Cyclone Julia is heading this way."

People started yelling questions and comments.

"If you live on the Tablelands, you have time to go home. I suggest you leave *now*. Put your cyclone plans into action," said Jay. "Everyone else, please follow my instructions. This is for your own safety."

Some people got in cars and started engines.

"Wait!" Jay called through the loudspeaker. "There is no need to panic. I repeat, there is no need to panic. We have about two hours to prepare. Please listen carefully. If you don't live on the Tablelands, do *not* try to leave. We have a safety plan."

Jay called for volunteers to help. "Secure your own vehicles first," he said. "Then we'll organize help for others. There is no need to panic. I repeat, there is no need to panic."

James picked up Ace to stop her howling. Then he turned to Tina, who had come out of a van close by with Pipwen in her arms. "Why does everyone panic when they're told there's no need to panic?" he said as he looked around. "That tree is too close to us. I think we should drive into the open. Can you please look after Ace while I pack our tent?"

Tina took Ace back to her van. I watched James take down our tent. Then he drove the Fourby to the clearest area we could find. "You stay with Tina and Ace," he said to me as we walked back to Tina's van. "I'm going to help other people pack up."

I didn't want to stay with Tina. For once, though, there was nothing I could do. I can run, jump, track, herd and chase, but I can't pack tents.

In the van, Tina had Pipwen on her lap. Ace was whining and scraping at the door.

"It's all right, Ace," I said. "James will come and get us soon." I really hoped he would.

It was a scary time for us because we didn't know what was happening. Tina gave us a drink. Then she put Pipwen in a pet carrier while she piled up things she wanted to keep safe.

The van shook suddenly. It felt as if someone had given it a hard push.

"Whoa!" said Tina.

Pipwen yelped. "I'm scared!"

I was scared too. I tucked my tail down and moved closer to Ace. Tina is my friend. Pipwen is a border collie, like me. But Ace is part of my pack, so she was the one I had to look after. I wished James would hurry.

The van shook again. Outside, we heard a few bangs and some yells.

By the time James came back, things were getting scarier. He put his head into the van. His hair was blowing all over the place. "Time to go to the woolshed," he said. "Give me Pipwen's basket and your sleeping bag, Tina."

"What about Stamp and Ace?"

"Emergency hands-free leashes," said

James. He snapped on our leashes and clipped the other ends to his belt. Then he picked up the pet carrier with Pipwen crying inside.

"You should get your stuff from the Fourby," said Tina.

"I already took that over to the woolshed. Come on."

Another gust of wind hit the van and made it shake and shudder. We got out of the van and walked slowly towards the big woolshed. The wind was blowing so hard my tail blew right around my side and my ears hurt. Ace kept close to me. Her hair blew into her eyes.

The air was full of things flying around. Bits of paper, bark, branches and clothing slammed against the parked vans and cars. Most of the tents had been taken down, but we saw one blow over and wrap around a man who was carrying a scared terrier.

James untangled the man. "Hurry!" he said. We all rushed the last few steps to the woolshed.

Jay and another steward were waiting to close the heavy doors. "You okay, James?" he asked. He checked off our names on a list.

"Sure," said James. "I'll just get the dogs settled. Is there anything I can do?"

"Go around and make sure everyone has secured their animals. A lot of these dogs have never been in a cyclone before and they'll panic. Now that I've marked you off my list, please *don't* go out again. If your dogs need a toilet break, take them to the sheep pen over in that corner. We've laid down sawdust."

"Who do I report to?" asked James.

"Any of the stewards. We're all members of the **Civil Defense**. Here . . ." Jay slapped a sticker on James's shirt. "That's a volunteer badge."

The woolshed walls were thick, so as soon as the doors shut, the sound of the wind was muffled. It seemed very still, but I could smell how frightened everyone was. People milled around, looking for friends or family members. Some dogs were running loose.

James took Ace and me to a corner where his sleeping bag and our blankets were already laid out. The tent was there in its bag, along with our supplies and the radio. James had gotten almost everything out of the Fourby. Maureen and Blue were next to us. Tina and Pipwen settled down on the other side.

"Blue heelers are brave," said Blue. "Some other dogs will panic, though."

"Yes," I agreed. I had been looking forward to the K9 Festival. Now it looked like our scariest adventure yet.

Stamp's Glossary

Civil Defense. A group of people who help out during emergencies.
Loudspeaker. A thing dog shows and other gatherings have so people and dogs can hear instructions.

Chapter Six

Where's Ace?

The air was still and hot inside the
woolshed, but we heard the roaring
outside. It went on and on, sometimes
dropping but always rising again. James
and I helped people catch frightened
dogs that had escaped in the panic.
Because I am a border collie, I am good
at herding. I rounded up dogs and other
animals and kept them still so James could
catch them. I felt better now that I had

something useful to do. Helping James is an important part of my life as top dog of the Fourby Pack.

Maureen and Jay's wife, Hayley, were with the stewards and volunteers, making sandwiches and tea.

"The power will go soon," said Hayley as she handed James a mug of tea. "The phones went down half an hour ago."

"Is there a **generator**?" asked James.

"Yes," said Hayley. "Jay's got two on standby, but they were never meant to carry this much load. It's just plain bad luck to have a cyclone with so many extra people at Atherton Tops." Just then, we heard a terrible crunch outside that went on and on.

"What's that?" asked Maureen.

"I don't know." Hayley had to raise her voice. "It could be the roof of one of the barns coming down."

"I hope you don't want me to check?" asked James.

"No! Now that we're under cover, we have to stay here until we get the all clear. This could be a long day."

James and I headed back to our spot. On the way, an older man stopped us. "You're a volunteer, young man?"

"Yes," said James. "Can I help you?"

"My name's Grig. Do you know if there's a vet in the building?"

"I don't know." James looked at the old man's two dogs. One was a spaniel and the other, a terrier mix. She looked a lot like Ace, except she was fatter. She was panting and pushing her bedding around with her nose. "Is she all right?" asked James, pointing to her. "It looks as if she's about to have pups."

"She is," said the old man. "My daughter works long hours so there's no one at home to look after Tilly. That's why I brought her along. The pups aren't due until next week, but I think she's going to have them early. I'd like a—"

The rest of what the old man said was lost in an even louder crash from outside.

I went to the little dog and gave her a nose-over. "Are you okay, Tilly?" I asked.

She went on pushing her bedding. "I must make a nest for my pups. It's got to be right."

"If there isn't a vet, I can help," said James. "My dad breeds border collies, so I've helped out with a lot of litters."

"It'll be a while yet," said Mr. Grig.

"Okay," said James. "I'll come back a bit later."

We went back to our spot to check on
Ace, but we couldn't see her.

"Ace!" called James.

Ace didn't come.

"Tina, have you seen Ace?" asked
James.

Tina had Pipwen on her lap and she
looked up. "She's under her blanket, I
think. She burrowed in during that loud
noise."

Ace's blanket was all humped up.
James put his hand on it. I expected Ace
to growl, but she wasn't underneath.

"Well, she *was* there," said Tina.

"She must have sneaked out. I hope
she's not bothering anyone. Stamp?
Where's Ace?"

I know Ace's scent, so I sniffed around until I found her trail.

It took me a while to track Ace's trail. She'd been running around a lot. I think she was tracking James and me because her trail went past people we'd helped.

"Where is she?" said James as I stopped and **cast about**. "Ace!"

I ignored James because I was busy tracking. I knew she was close by, but somehow the scent I smelled wasn't quite right.

I trotted over to a group of children playing with a teddy bear. I hoped Ace hadn't gone there. They might have tried to pat her and Ace is as unpredictable as a cyclone. She might grab their toy and run.

I pushed my nose pawlitely between two children. One of them giggled.

"Hello, Stamp!"

It was Imogen. I wagged my tail and she patted me. Then she turned to the small boy beside her. "It's my turn."

The boy handed over the teddy bear. It was a big fluffy one, with silky flowing hair.

As Imogen gathered it into her arms, it made a contented **grungle**.

That's when I realized it wasn't a teddy bear at all. It was Ace!

Stamp's Glossary

Cast about. Trotted back and forth, looking for a clue.

Generator. A portable machine that generates electricity.

Grungle. A happy little growl.

Chapter Seven
Ace's Fan Club

"Ace! What are you doing?" I asked.

Ace was lying upside down in Imogen's arms waving her front paws. When she heard me, she wriggled the right way up. She peered at me over Imogen's shoulder.

"What do you want, Stamp?" she asked. Her hair looked soft and silky and she had a red bow tied up on top of her head. Even her toenails gleamed. She smelled of Pooch Polish.

"I was looking for you," I said. "James is worried about you."

Ace sniffed. "I'm surprised he even noticed I was missing." She licked Imogen's ear.

"Come on, Ace," I said.

"No," she said.

Imogen picked up a comb and gently combed Ace's neck. Ace sighed. "Treat?" she said, wagging her tail.

Imogen took a treat from her pocket and held it out. Ace took it pawlitely and crunched it up. "Go away, Stamp," she said. "You left me."

"Ace, catch!" said the little boy. He tossed her a piece of cheese and Ace snapped it out of the air.

The children laughed. "Clever doggie," said the boy.

Ace swallowed the cheese and polished her whiskers, then snuggled up to Imogen.

"We didn't just leave you. You were all right with Tina. James and I have been helping and herding," I said. "There was nothing you could do."

"Of-paws there is. I'm helping these little kids right now," said Ace. "They think they're teaching me tricks. It keeps them from being so scared."

James came up then. Like me, he had a

56

hard time recognizing Ace. It wasn't only that she was fluffy and wearing a ribbon. It was the way she was acting.

"There you are, Ace!" he said. Then he recognized Imogen. "Hello, Imogen. What are you doing with Ace?"

"Making her pretty," said Imogen.

"Your daddy told you not to pat dogs without permission. You do know some dogs might bite you, right?"

"You said I could pat Ace later," said Imogen. "It's later now."

"Okay," said James. He clicked his fingers. "Ace, are you coming?"

Ace squinted at him. "No. I'm helping these kids."

I couldn't get her to come with us. Of-paws, James could have picked her up and carried her back to our spot, but he didn't. I suppaws he knew if he tied her up, she'd nose-whinge. If he didn't, she'd just come back to the children.

"Come on, Stamp," he said. "We'd better go. She'll come when she's ready." He laughed. "She can't get out of the woolshed. She seems to be having a lovely time with her **fan club**."

As James spoke, there was another terrible crunch from outside. The wind howled and the whole building shook.

I looked back at Ace. She was snuggled in Imogen's arms. I whined, but I don't think James heard me.

We went to tell Tina we'd found Ace and then back to Tilly and her owner. The wind was screaming too loudly for James to talk to the old man, but we could see Tilly was having her pups. One puppy had already been born. He was wet and sticky. I saw his pink mouth open to squeak, but I didn't hear it.

James picked up an old towel and gently picked up the new puppy. He rubbed his fur with the towel and looked at his nose and mouth. His eyes were shut. James put him down next to Tilly and he snuggled against her. Soon another pup was born, and then another one. James helped Tilly dry each one, checked it over and then put it back beside her.

In the end, there were five pups. Four were not much bigger than mice. One was quite a bit bigger. They were patched black and brown and white like Tilly. The big one was nearly all white. They had pink paws and pink noses and mouths. I know they were all squeaking, but I couldn't hear them.

Tilly saw me looking and darted her

head at me. I couldn't hear her, either, but I knew what she wanted to say. *Move back or I'll nip you.*

I moved back a bit. It's not a good idea to bother a mother dog when she has a new **litter**.

Tilly gave me another look and then seemed to forget all about me. James spread a clean towel in her bed and moved her onto it. Soon the pups were all cuddled up drinking milk.

James filled a water dish for Tilly. Mother dogs need to drink lots of water. Then he smiled at Mr. Grig and gave him the thumbs-up sign.

Suddenly, things changed. James rubbed his ears. "Has it suddenly gone quiet?" he said.

It *had* gone quiet. Instead of howling and crashes, I heard the pups sucking, the spaniel licking his paws and someone coughing.

Was the cyclone over?

Hayley hit an empty pot with a spoon until everyone stopped talking and looked at her.

Jay came up beside her. "Listen up, everyone! As you hear, the wind has dropped. I know you're all anxious to see how your vehicles survived the storm, but *please* stay inside. Cyclone Julia has not finished with us yet. This is the eye of the cyclone. It will be quiet for a little while. Then it will be back."

Mr. Grig sighed. "I bet my daughter's worried. The phones are all down, so I can't call her."

"If you give me her name and number, I can get my dad to call her for you," said James. "The radio will work once I hook it up to the battery and the HF antenna."

Mr. Grig wrote down the name and number. "Kelly is a reporter," he said. "This is her work number."

James set up the RF radio and called Barnaby Station. Dad Barnaby answered right away.

"What's happening, James? Over."

"All safe in the woolshed at Atherton Tops," said James. "All well, though I don't know about the Fourby. Over."

"Glad all's okay. Over," said Dad Barnaby.

"Dad, do you have a pen? Can you call this number and tell Kelly Grig her dad's okay and so is everyone else? She's a reporter. She'll get the news out on a news broadcast. Over."

"Copy that, James. Over."

James read out the number to Dad

Barnaby.

We all jumped as a crash came from outside.

"The cyclone's on its way back," said James. "I'll sign off now, Dad."

I don't know if Dad Barnaby said anything more because the wind came back with a loud howl.

Stamp's Glossary

Fan club. A group of people who are all interested in the same thing.
Litter. Family of pups or kittens.

Chapter Eight
Where's Imogen?

The wind howled for a long time. A lot of the dogs were upset, but there was nothing we could do. Cyclone Julia screamed around Atherton Tops for a whole day and half the night. It was hard to keep track of time. At last the howls stopped. Most people were so tired they just lay down to sleep.

Jay opened the woolshed door. He shone a flashlight out into the rain.

"How is it?" asked James. I peered out between his legs and breathed in gulps of damp air. I smelled raw earth and rain.

"Too dark to tell," said Jay. "There will be a huge mess out there, but no one was hurt. That's the main thing." He pushed the doors closed again. "We'll have to stay in here until morning, anyway. It would be crazy to go out there in the dark."

"Yes," said James. "And it's taught me one thing."

"What's that?" asked Jay.

"Next time my dad says there's a cyclone heading in my direction, I'll go the other way!"

Jay laughed. "Cyclones come and go in the tropics. This one wasn't one of the worst, thank goodness."

"I'd hate to see one that was worse than that," said James.

"It was a Category 3, I reckon. The big ones are Category 5. Well, I'm off for a nap. Immo must be bedded down with Hayley. I won't disturb them."

James and I went back to our beds. Ace was curled up under a heap of blanket with her sharp little nose sticking out of the pile. I didn't wake her. She was still wearing the bow.

We slept for a few hours. When I opened my eyes again, I saw a streak of daylight coming from the big doors. Jay must have gone outside to look around.

I yawned and stretched my legs. Then I had a good scratch and a lap from my water bowl. After that, I looked over to see if James and Ace were awake.

James was still sleeping. Ace's blanket was scratched up in a hump as usual. I had a good sniff, but she wasn't there.

Now where is she? I wondered. I was about to track her down when James stretched and opened his eyes. "Hi, Stamp." He reached out to rub my ears. "Hi, Ace." He put his hand out to the lump in her blanket, but it just squashed down.

"Not again!" James yawned. "I should have tied her up. I suppose she's gone off with her fan club."

Tina was up feeding Pipwen some kibble. "It's all over, then?" she said when she saw that James was awake.

"I think Jay's looking around out there now," said James. "We'd better wait for the all clear before we go out."

"I want a cup of tea," said Tina. "Is Ace back?"

"She was here last night," said James. "Now she's gone back to her fan club. It's really odd."

Tina laughed. "Some dogs like kids."

"I know, but I had no idea Ace was one of them."

They went off to see about breakfast. On the way, I stopped to check up on Tilly and her pups. They were all asleep. So were Mr. Grig and the spaniel. I didn't go too close.

I missed Ace. Ever since we first met her at Cousin Jeannie's place, she had been with me almost all the time. Now James had gone off with Tina and Pipwen, and Ace was away with her fan club. I felt lonely. I wanted them both back. I wanted to be driving along in the Fourby with my pack.

"You're getting pawfully pawsessive, Stamp," I told myself. "That's not good." I lifted my nose and sniffed around, then I went off after James.

Hayley was serving coffee and tea, but she looked worried. "Have you seen Imogen?" she asked. "She was with me all night, but I haven't seen her this morning."

"She's probably playing with Ace again," said James. "We'll go and find them." He looked down at me. "Stamp? Where's Ace?"

I cast about. Ace had been running all over the woolshed, so it wasn't easy to find her trail.

After a minute, we heard the loudspeaker again. "Imogen! Imogen Alan! Where are you?" It was Hayley's voice. She sounded worried.

A minute later, Jay rushed in through the big doors. He hurried up to Hayley and I saw them talking. Then Jay took the loudspeaker. "Attention, everyone! Some of you know our daughter, Imogen. If anyone can see her, please let us know. She's wearing overalls and a yellow shirt."

Soon nearly everyone was looking for Imogen. Before long, it was clear that she wasn't in the woolshed.

Neither was Ace.

James looked really worried. "Stamp, find Ace!" he said. Then he went to Jay. "Is it safe to go outside? My dog's missing."

Jay frowned distractedly at him. "I'm sorry. I'm too worried about my child to worry about your dog. If you go looking outside, just take care." He turned back to the other stewards and we heard him organizing a search party.

"You can't blame him," said Tina. "Ace is important to you, but Imogen is just a little girl."

"I *know* that!" snapped James.

My heart seemed to sink. James hardly ever snaps. He always finds what is best to do and does it.

Chapter Nine
On The Trail

I cast about near the door and suddenly
I picked up a fresh scent. I ran back to
paw at James's leg. Then I ran back to the
door.

The rain had stopped, but there was
a terrible mess. Branches and tents lay all
over the place. One of the barns had lost
its roof, which had landed on top of one
of the challenge walkways. All the canoes
were smashed up in the dam and one had

blown halfway across the paddock. Vans were rammed into one another.

For a moment, I had no idea what to do. Then I took a deep sniff of the fresh air. The first thing to do was find Ace. She was part of my pack.

I sniffed around and soon I found her trail. All the other dog smells had washed away in the storm so it was easy to track her. I trotted along and started to feel confident. I can do this! I told myself.

I trotted past broken vans and torn tents towards where we had camped. Ace came this way. She must have been looking for the Fourby.

That's when I saw the huge tree we had parked under. It had blown down in the cyclone and now it lay smashed and broken all over the ground.

And Ace's trail headed straight for it.

What if Ace was under there? How could I bear it if we lost her?

I put back my head and howled. I howled and howled. Then I had to stop for breath.

As I started scraping at the edge of the broken branches, I heard a cranky yap.

"Ace!"

Ace yapped again.

"Ace!" I scraped harder. "Are you hurt?"

"About time you came, Stamp," said Ace's voice. "I'm not hurt, but I can't come out. I have to look after Imogen."

"I'll get you out—"

"Don't be silly, Stamp," said Ace. "Get James. This is a job for a pack leader."

I raced back to the woolshed. I felt as if I had wings on my paws. James was calling me, so I dashed up to him and pranced my paws. I jumped around, barking.

James grinned. "You found her! Where?"

I took off back to the tree and James raced after me. I won, of-paws. A fit young border collie can outrun humans.

I skidded to a stop near the fallen tree and barked.

"Ace!" called James.

Ace yapped back.

Then we heard a little voice. "Is that you, James?"

"Imogen?" James pushed as far as he could into the branches. "Are you all right?"

"I can't get out!"

"It's okay, Immo. Stay still. I'll leave Stamp here. I'll get your dad and mum! Can you wait just a minute?"

"Ace is with me. I'm okay."

James ran off and in a few minutes the

rescue team arrived.

The stewards and volunteers worked together and soon they had the broken roots pulled away. Imogen and Ace were in the hole where the tree roots were. The roots were still attached to the earth, so the tree, which had blown over, had begun to drop back into its original position.

Jay said afterward it was lucky we found them when we did. The tree could have flipped back at any time.

As soon as the roots were clear, Ace hopped out of the hole. Jay lifted Imogen up and hugged her, earth and all.

"Immo, what happened?"

Imogen looked around. "Sorry, Daddy. I woke up and the big wind had stopped. I wanted to play with Ace in the fort, but the tree had fallen down. I thought maybe we could make another fort in the hole where the tree was and then I got stuck."

I looked at Ace. "You shouldn't have gone out without James and me."

"I had to make sure Imogen was okay," said Ace. "I knew you'd come and find me."

Chapter Ten

The Great Atherton Kq and Friends Festival

Atherton Tops was all messed up after the cyclone. James, Tina and Maureen joined the volunteers and helped with the big cleanup. As James said, we might as well because we had to wait for the Fourby to be fixed. The tree hadn't fallen on it because James moved it before the cyclone, but it had some damage from flying debris.

After a while, things were back to

normal. And guess what? The Great Atherton K9 and Friends Festival went ahead after all! It was a few weeks late and a lot of people had already gone home, but the locals and the volunteers said they wanted some fun.

By now, Tina's Pipwen was old enough to compete in the puppy class. James and I entered the sheepdog trial, the best-trained dog and, of course, the big challenge. The canoes were all broken, so we had to swim across the dam instead, but the ladders and pipes and balance beams were all back in place. It was pawfully good. I'd never had so much fun!

Imogen asked James if she could enter Ace in the under seven class. "I want to make her feel special. Daddy says winning isn't important. We do contests for fun."

That's how James, Tina, Pipwen,

Maureen, Blue, Mr. Grig and his spaniel, Jay and Hayley and Mr. Grig's daughter Kelly came to see Ace win a blue ribbon! I don't know who was the most surprised.

Kelly took a photo for the newspaper and James kept the paper to show Mum and Dad Barnaby. We still have the picture. In it, Imogen is laughing and Ace has a smug smarl.

It was all great, but I had a sad feeling in my heart. Ace and Imogen got along so well that I thought James and I would be leaving Atherton Tops alone.

On the last day, James packed up the Fourby with all of our gear. "Come on, dogs," he said. He opened the back door for me and Ace.

Imogen knelt down and cuddled Ace. Then she started to cry. "I don't want Ace to go," she sobbed.

Mr. Grig was there to say good-bye to us. "Come over to my van," he said to Imogen. "There's someone who would like to meet you."

We all went over and Mr. Grig opened the back of his van. Inside was a basket. Tilly sat in it with her five pups. They had grown a lot, and now their eyes were open. The biggest one was trying to climb out of the basket. Mr. Grig picked him up. The puppy gave a little growl and then yawned.

"This young man will soon be looking for a good home," said Mr. Grig. "In about four weeks, he'll be ready to leave his mum. Do you think you could look after him, Imogen?"

Imogen went on hugging Ace, but she put out one hand to stroke the puppy. Then she looked at Jay and Hayley. "Mum?"

Hayley nodded. "If you like him, he can be yours, Immo."

Imogen nodded. "I love Ace, but I guess she wants to go with James and Stamp." She gave Ace one last cuddle and put her down. Ace licked her hand and then ran off and jumped into the back of the Fourby.

Ten minutes later, we were on the road again, heading for our next adventure.

"I was afraid you'd want to stay with

Imogen," I said to Ace.

"I like her," said Ace, "but you and James are my pack." Then she scraped the back of James's seat with her claws. "Are we there yet?"

A Word on Storm and Cyclone Safety for Pets

Severe storms and cyclones are frightening, so don't forget your pets. If your animal friends usually live outside, make sure they have strong wind- and waterproof kennels or houses for normal wet or windy weather. If the storm is a bad one, try to bring pets inside. If you have indoor pets, keep them with you in the safest part of the house.

Remember, if it's not safe for you to be outside, it's not safe for your pets, either. They rely on you to keep them calm and as comfortable as possible.

Join Stamp, Ace and James in their other Pup Patrol adventures!

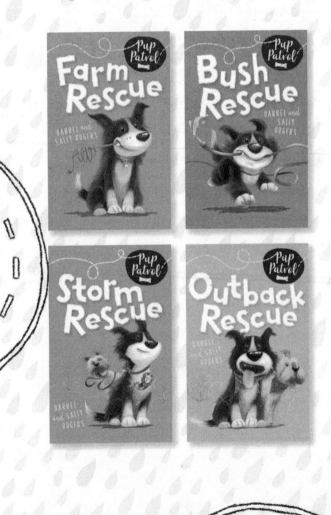